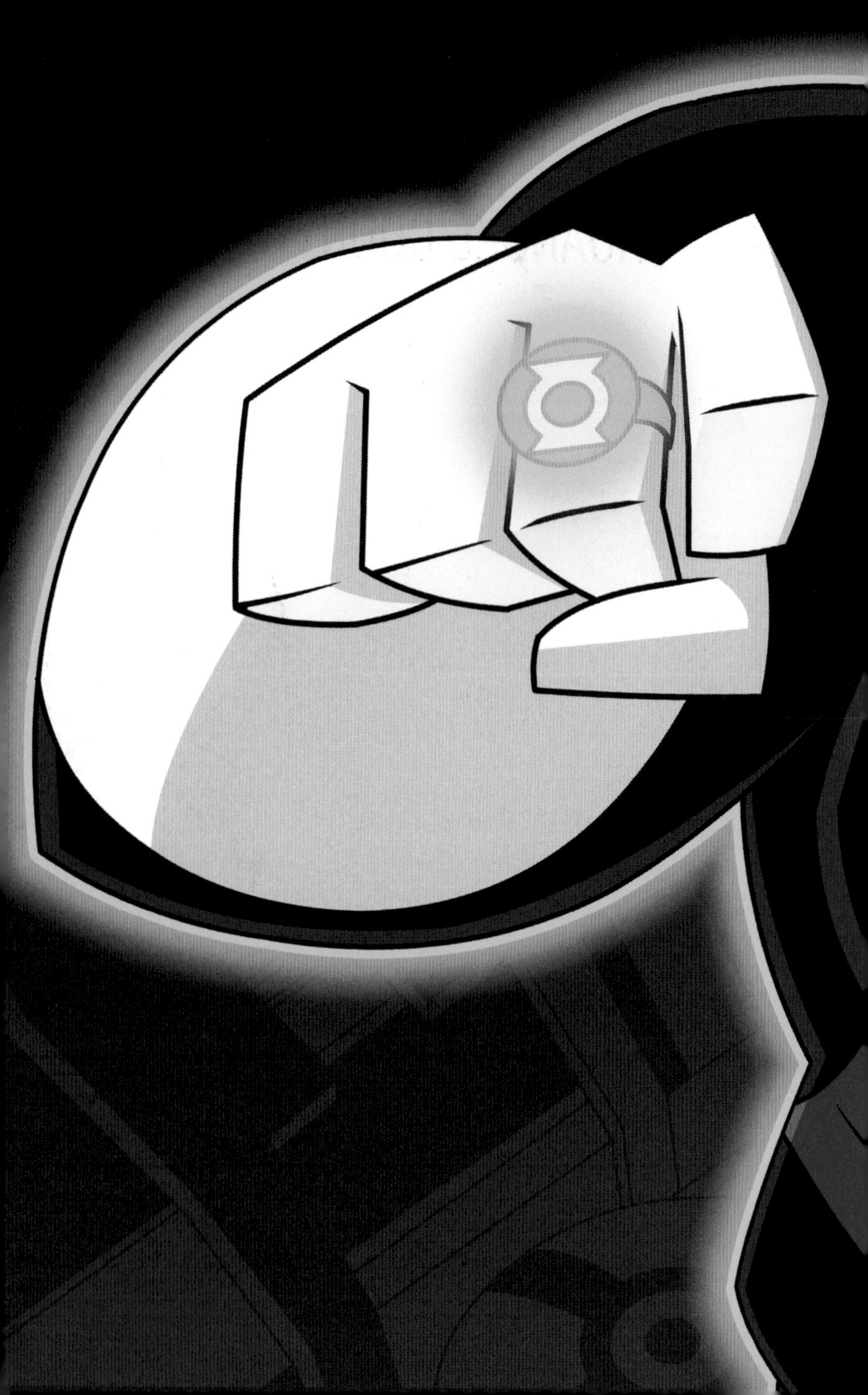

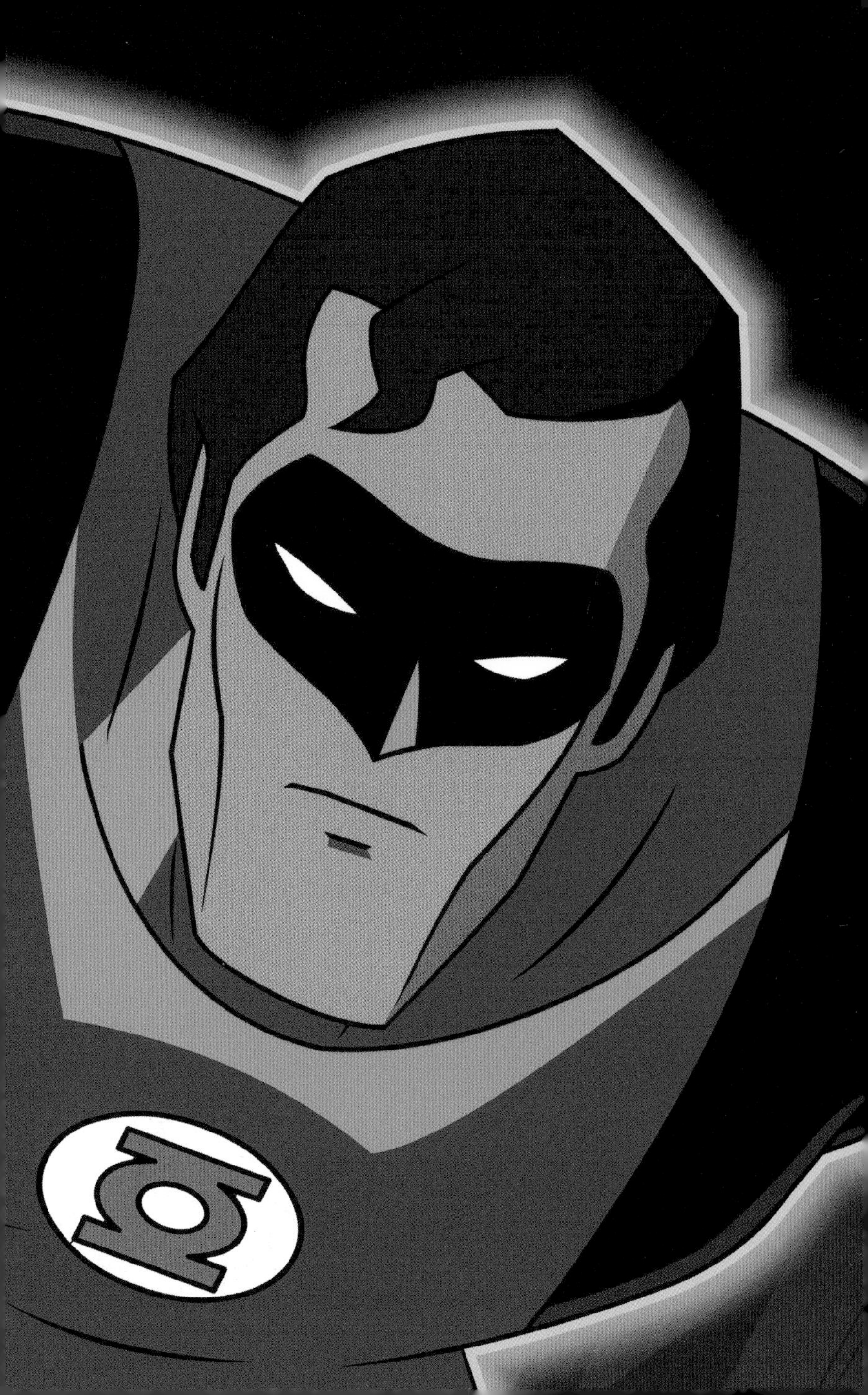

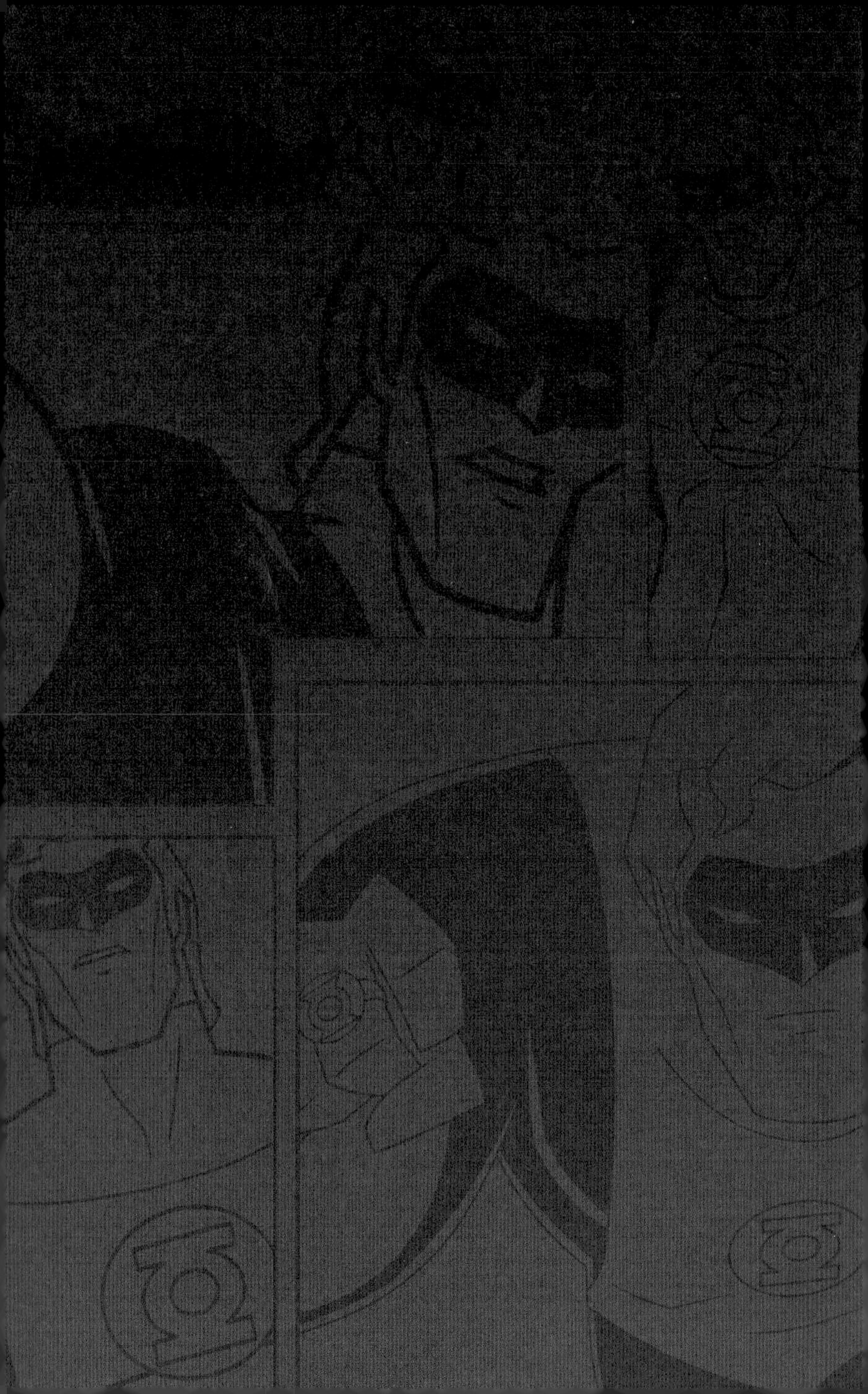

AS THE NEWEST MEMBER OF AN INTERGALACTIC PEACEKEEPING FORCE KNOWN AS THE GREEN LANTERN CORPS, HAL JORDAN FIGHTS EVIL AND PROUDLY WEARS THE UNIFORM AND RING OF . . .

SUPER DC HEROES™

GREEN LANTERN™

GUARDIAN OF EARTH

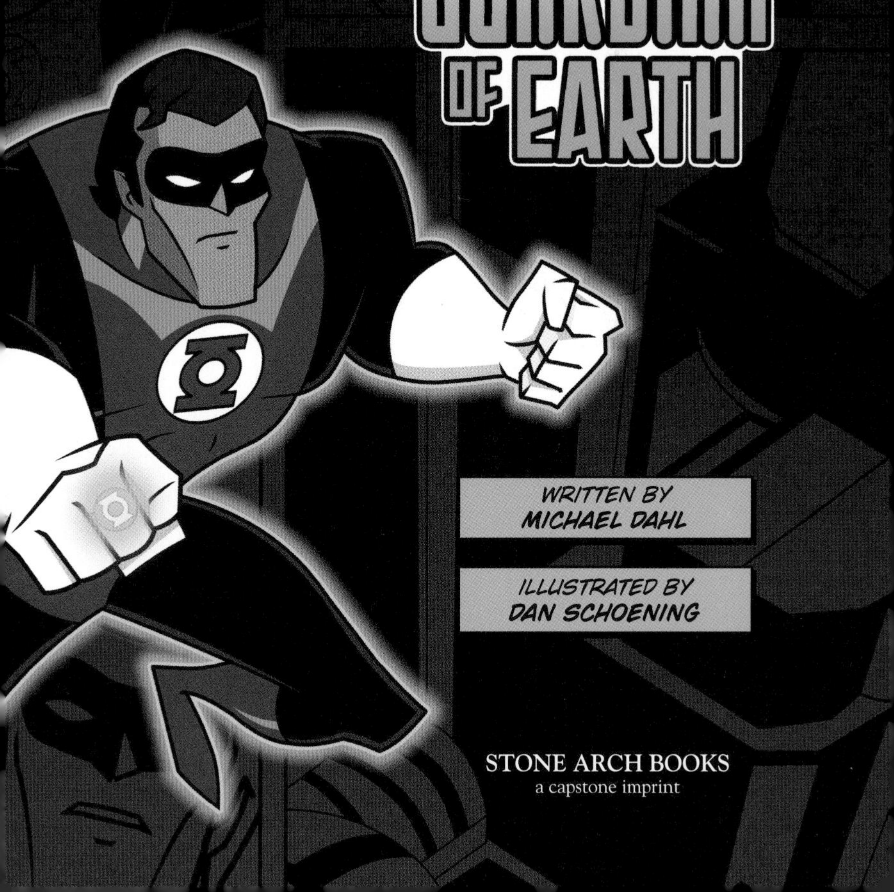

WRITTEN BY
MICHAEL DAHL

ILLUSTRATED BY
DAN SCHOENING

STONE ARCH BOOKS
a capstone imprint

Published by Stone Arch Books in 2011
A Capstone Imprint
151 Good Counsel Drive, P.O. Box 669
Mankato, Minnesota 56002
www.capstonepub.com

Library of Congress Cataloging-in-Publication Data

Dahl, Michael.
  Guardian of Earth / written by Michael Dahl ; illustrated by Dan Schoening.
    p. cm. -- (DC super heroes. Green Lantern)
  ISBN 978-1-4342-2611-2 (library binding) -- ISBN 978-1-4342-3081-2 (pbk.)
  1. Graphic novels. [1. Graphic novels. 2. Superheroes--Fiction.] I. Schoening,
Dan, ill. II. Title.
  PZ7.7.D34Gu 2011
  741.5'973--dc22   2010025600

Summary: During a routine test flight above the deserts of the Southwest, ace
pilot Hal Jordan has a too-close-for-comfort encounter with a UFO. His jet
takes a nosedive, but before Hal bites the dust, a strange green glow appears
and prevents the crash. The mysterious UFO reveals Hal's alien rescuer,
who possesses a green ring of untold power. What does Hal do when the
alien offers him the ring and announces that the human pilot is now the new
Guardian of Earth?

Art Director: Bob Lentz
Designer: Hilary Wacholz
Production Specialist: Michelle Biedscheid

Printed in the United States of America in Stevens Point, Wisconsin.
092010
005934WZS11

TABLE of CONTENTS

CHAPTER 1

DESTINATION: EARTH 4

CHAPTER 2

TEST PILOT 11

CHAPTER 3

ABIN SUR 18

CHAPTER 4

POWER RING........................ 27

CHAPTER 5

GREEN LANTERN................... 36

DESTINATION: EARTH

Somewhere near the orbit of Mars, a small green craft hurtled at unthinkable speed. It flashed past the Martian moons of Phobos and Deimos. In moments, the dark disk of Earth's own moon filled up the viewing screen of the craft.

The ship's pilot made an adjustment at the controls. The ship abruptly turned. Then it curved around the face of the moon toward the bright side. Soon, another world came into view. A giant ball of blue and green grabbed the pilot's attention.

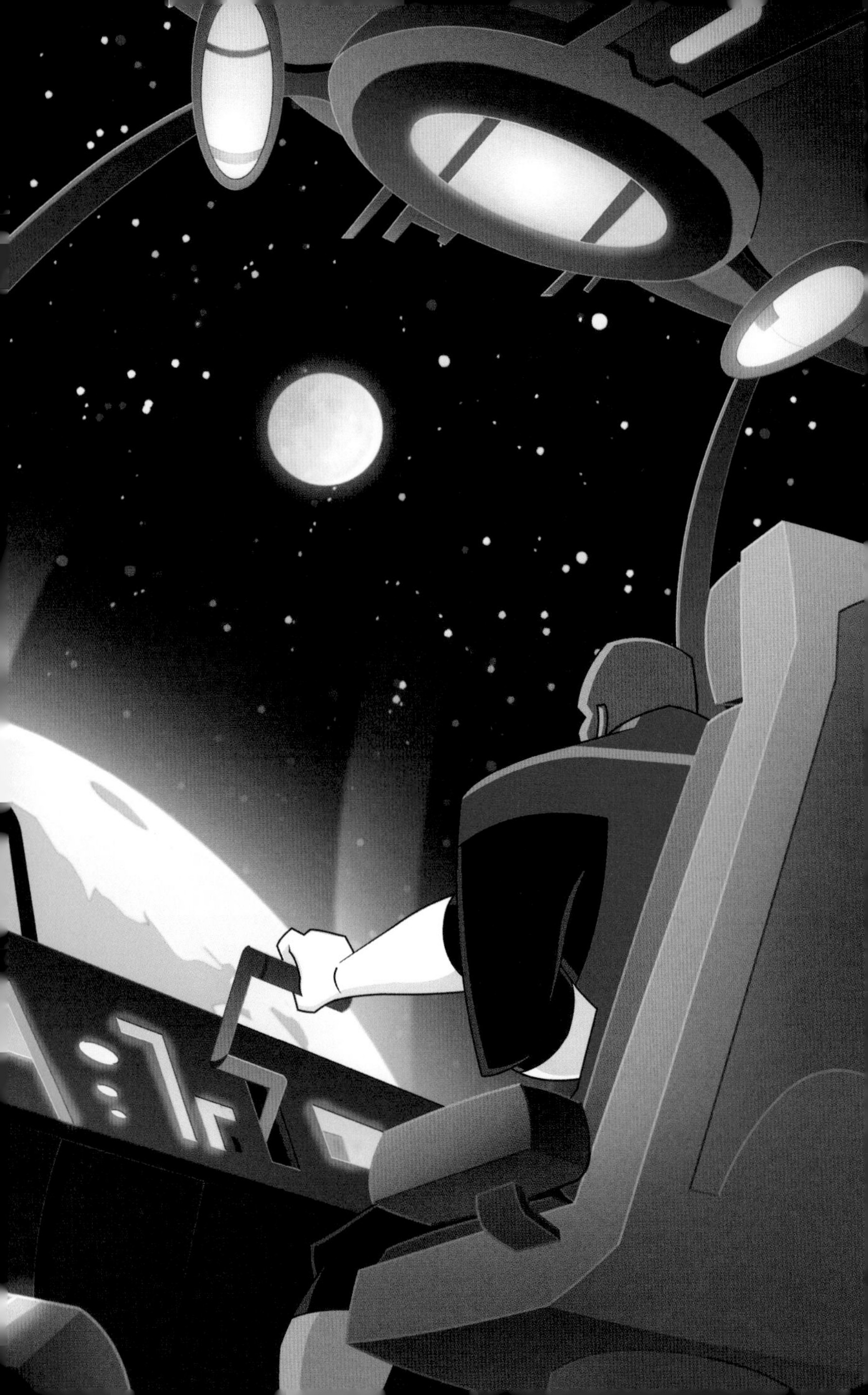

"Earth," whispered the pilot.

He did not speak the word for anyone else to hear. He was alone. He only said the planet's name because it gave him relief. He was nearing the end of his journey.

The pilot made another sound. A groan. He placed his hand against a severe wound on the side of his body. He only had a few minutes left to reach the surface of Earth. Otherwise it would be too late. The pilot stared down at the wound. Blood slowly oozed through his fingers.

WHOOOOSH!

The emerald ship cut through Earth's atmosphere. The angle of its flight changed once again, and it skimmed above the Pacific Ocean.

The pilot noticed a message flashing on his control deck: APPROACHING NORTH AMERICA.

Then the pilot lay back in his seat. He shut his eyes. He tried to forget the pain from his wound, even though it was terrible. Instead, he thought back to the moment just before he had been wounded. He relived the battle that had sent him on this journey halfway across the galaxy.

An outlaw starship had fired on him in a lonely section of the galaxy. He knew that a second blast from the outlaws would tear his ship apart, so the pilot soared away to safety.

A stab of pain had caused him to look downward.

There was a huge rip in his black and green uniform. He saw the wound in his side. It was deep. Small tendrils of energy were still pulsing inside of him, continuing to damage his internal organs.

Then the pilot raised his right hand. A green ring glowed on one of his fingers. The pilot concentrated. He thought of only one thing. *I am dying, but the ring cannot die,* he thought. *Someone else must wear it and learn its awesome power.* The pilot concentrated harder. *Someone with the ability to overcome great fear. But who is he?*

ZZRRRRTT! A beam of emerald light erupted from his ring. The beam thickened and turned into a column. The column grew into the figure of a human being. The human was a young man with wavy brown hair and strong eyes.

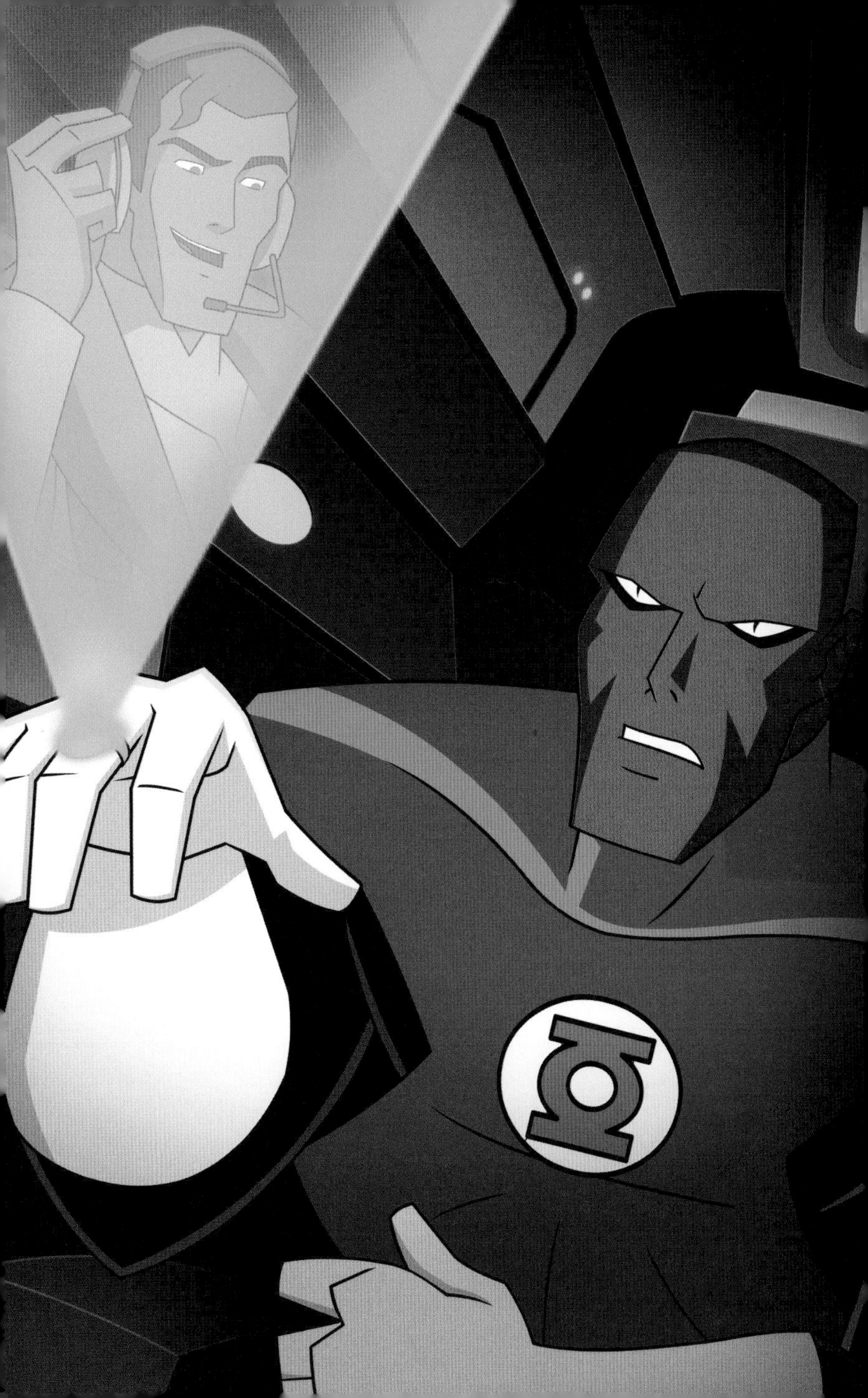

The man wore a one-piece flight suit. His name echoed inside the small ship as Abin Sur spoke the words.

"Hal Jordan," said the dying pilot.

As the emerald ship shot above the waves of the Pacific Ocean, the pilot from another world groaned. The blood continued to drain from his body. He lay back in his seat, waiting for the ship to reach its goal. He waited for the ring to locate its new owner.

He hoped he would find Hal Jordan in time.

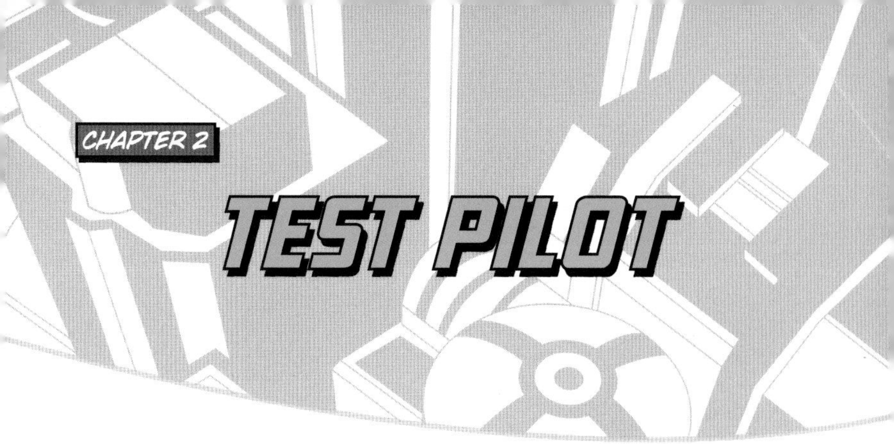

CHAPTER 2

TEST PILOT

Hal Jordan lifted up his helmet and goggles. Then a voice crackled over his headset. "Are you all right, Hal?" It was Carol Ferris speaking.

"Fine," said Hal. "My nose just itched."

Another sound came through the headset, but Hal couldn't make it out. Then Carol came back on. Her voice was louder this time.

"This is a test flight, Hal!" she said. "You can't take off your helmet."

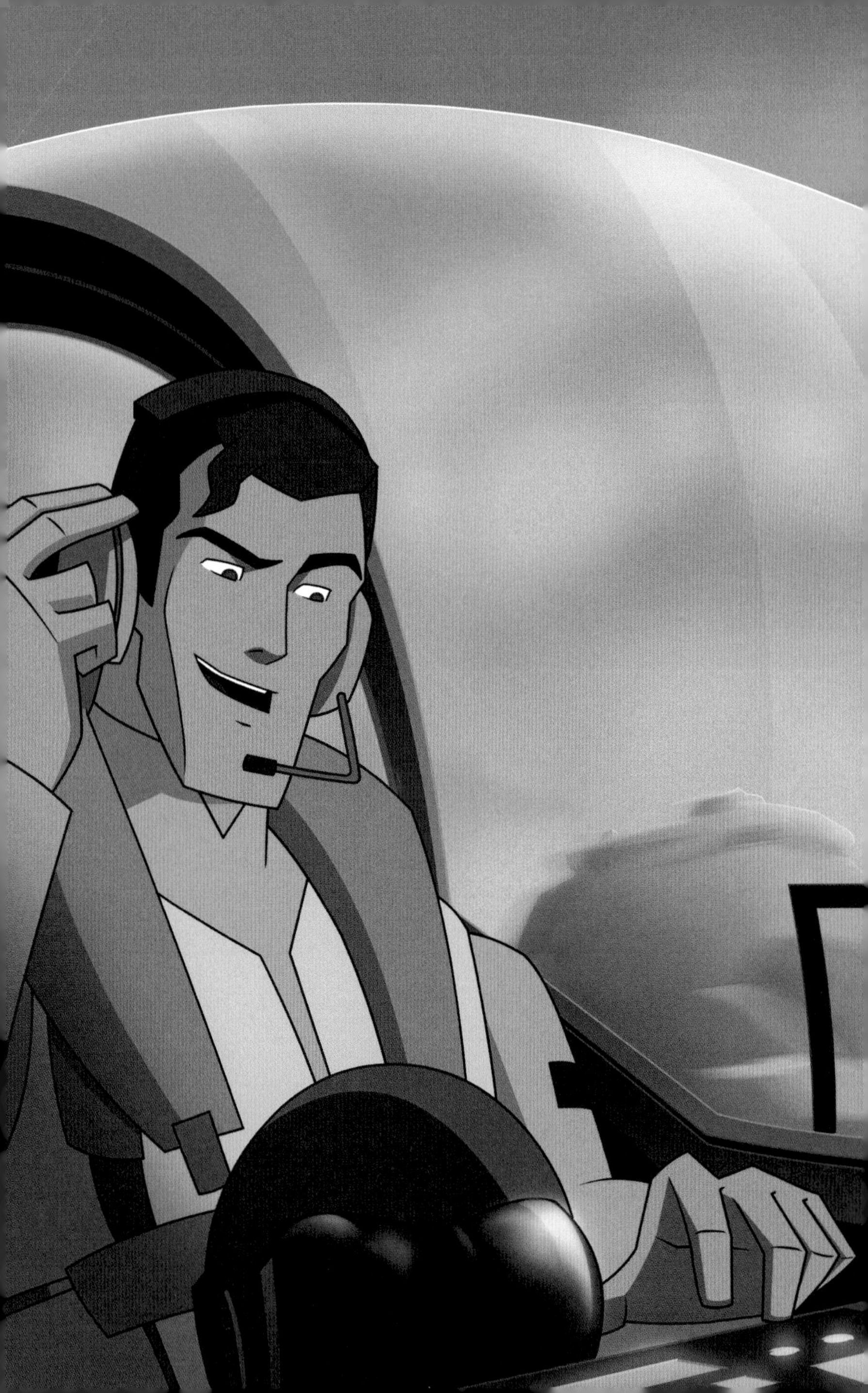

"No big deal," said Hal.

"Yes, it *is* a big deal," Carol said, firmly. "I'm the owner of this company, and I don't want you blacking out at 30,000 feet!"

Hal readjusted his helmet and checked his altimeter. "More like 41,000 feet," he said. He looked out the side of his cockpit. A sea of clouds lay far below him.

"You only have five minutes left on this run," said Carol. "You should start heading back now."

"Yes, ma'am," said Hal

A green blur rocketed past the nose of Hal's aircraft.

All the instrument lights in Hal's cockpit flashed off. "What the —?" he began.

RUMMMMMMMBLE! The jet wobbled and shook in the wake of the green blur.

"Hal!" shouted Carol. "What's going on?"

"I don't know," he said.

"We picked up some kind of disturbance in your area," she went on.

"No kidding," he said.

"Maybe a weather satellite, or —" The headset suddenly went dead.

For the next few moments, Hal tried rebooting the jet's system. No matter how many times he flipped switches, turned dials, and punched buttons, the control panel didn't respond.

"Great," Hal said to himself. "No instruments. No voice contact. No one to yell at me. What else could go wrong?"

Hal looked out at the burners. "At least we've got engine power," he said. Then he felt the fluttery feeling in his stomach that happens when a jet descends quickly.

One of the aircraft's burners coughed, sputtered, and died. Hal sighed. "Well, so much for engine power," he said.

Hal banked the jet sharply, trying to head back toward the airfield at Ferris Industries. "If I crash this thing, Carol is really going to be steamed," he joked.

The jet descended through the clouds. Hal could see the desert floor far beneath him, but it was moving up quickly.

The altimeter displayed the ship's rapid fall. 20,000 feet. 15,000 feet. 10,000 feet.

Hal worried that the acceleration and the shaking of the ship would cause him to black out before he could exit to safety. His right hand reached for the Eject button.

Suddenly, the ship slowed down. Hal's body was jerked forward. Then the jet completely stopped moving.

A weird green glow radiated through the cockpit panels. Hal looked outside. He couldn't believe his eyes.

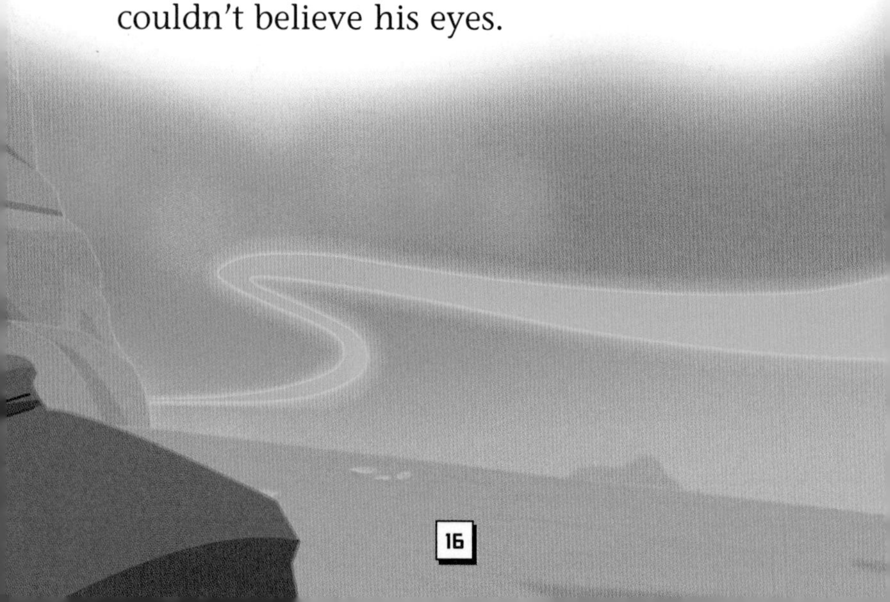

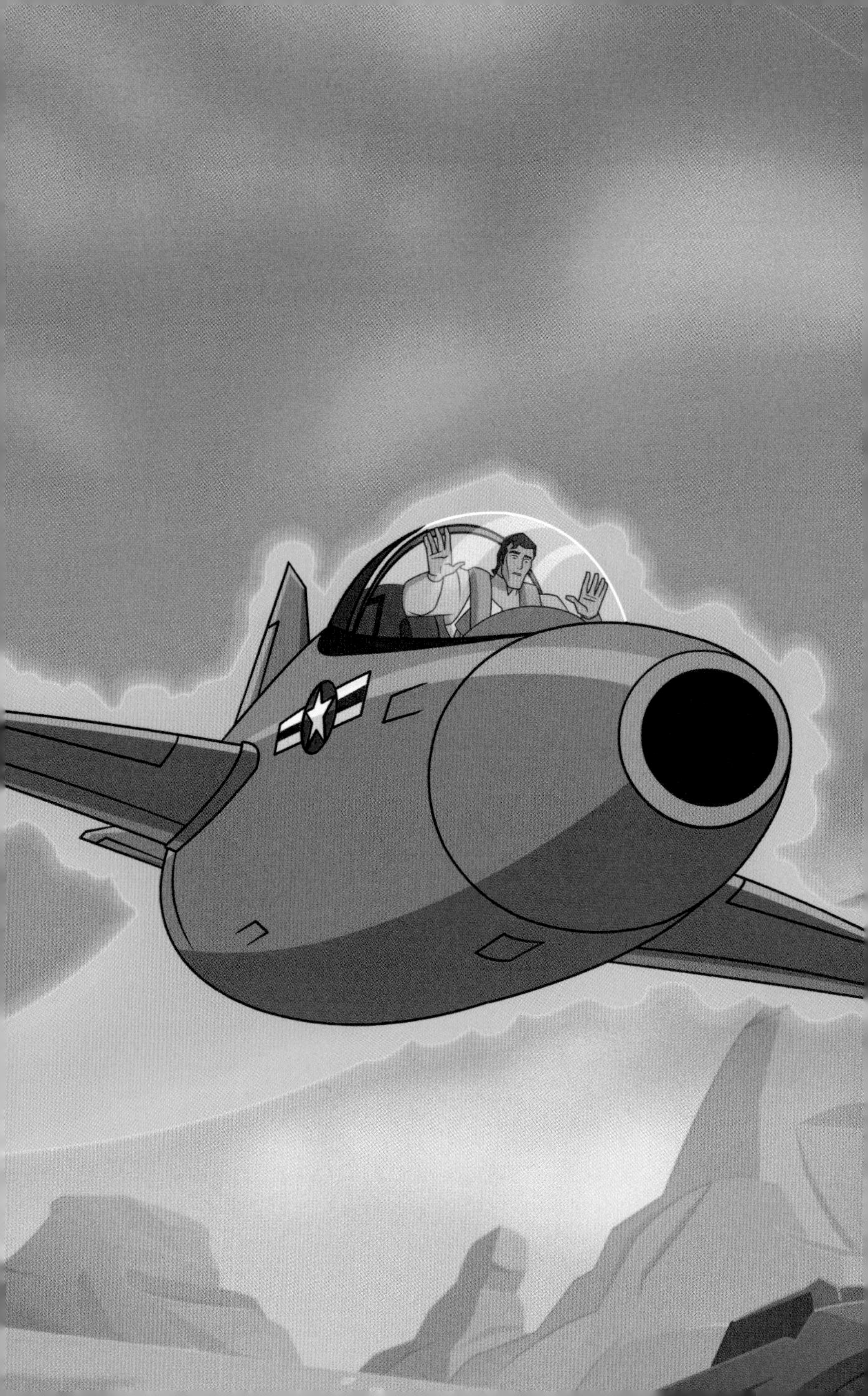

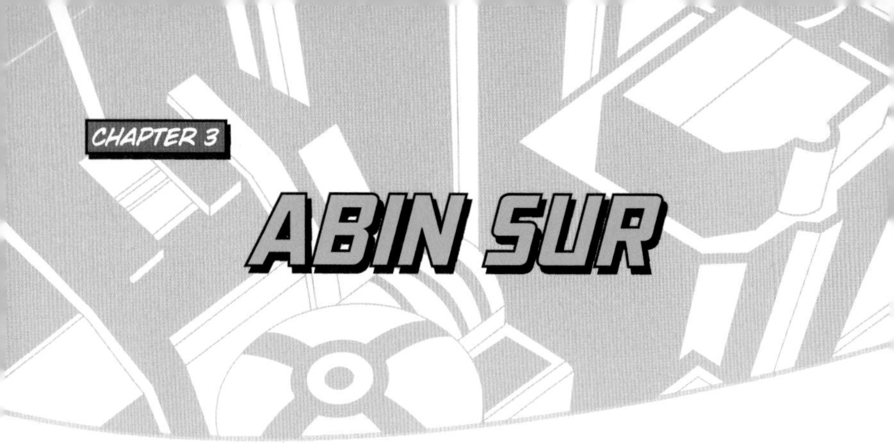

CHAPTER 3

ABIN SUR

I must be hallucinating, thought Hal. The jet gently rocked from side to side a few times. Then it lurched.

The test pilot blinked. The green glow under the ship disappeared. It was replaced by the reddish desert floor over which Hal had recently been flying. *Am I on the ground?* he wondered.

Hal raised the jet's canopy. Then he removed his helmet, untangled his six-foot frame from the pilot seat, and climbed out of the cockpit.

"Yup," he said. "I'm on the ground. But how?"

A hundred yards away, a cloud of thick black smoke rose from the rocks and sand. At first, Hal thought it was some part of his jet that had fallen off and crashed into the desert. Then he heard a voice.

Hal . . . Hal . . .

"Who's there?" called Hal.

Hal Jordan.

The test pilot walked toward the smoke. "Is someone here?" he shouted. Through the black clouds, Hal saw another ship. It was badly damaged.

Smoke poured out of a deep gash in the ship's green metallic side. *Green!* thought Hal. *This must have been the thing that flew past me.*

"Hello?!" he called out. Then he saw it.

A creature, about the same size and shape of a man, sat leaning against the ship. It had no hair. Its skin was the same color as the surrounding desert sand. The creature wore a strange uniform of black and green.

It's staring right at me, thought Hal.

Actually, I'm a he, not an it, came a voice inside Hal's brain. *I am of the male gender on my planet.*

"Your planet?" asked Hal.

"I am Abin Sur of Ungara," said the alien. "But not for much longer. I am badly injured and have only moments left before I join my ancestors."

"You need a doctor," said Hal, kneeling.

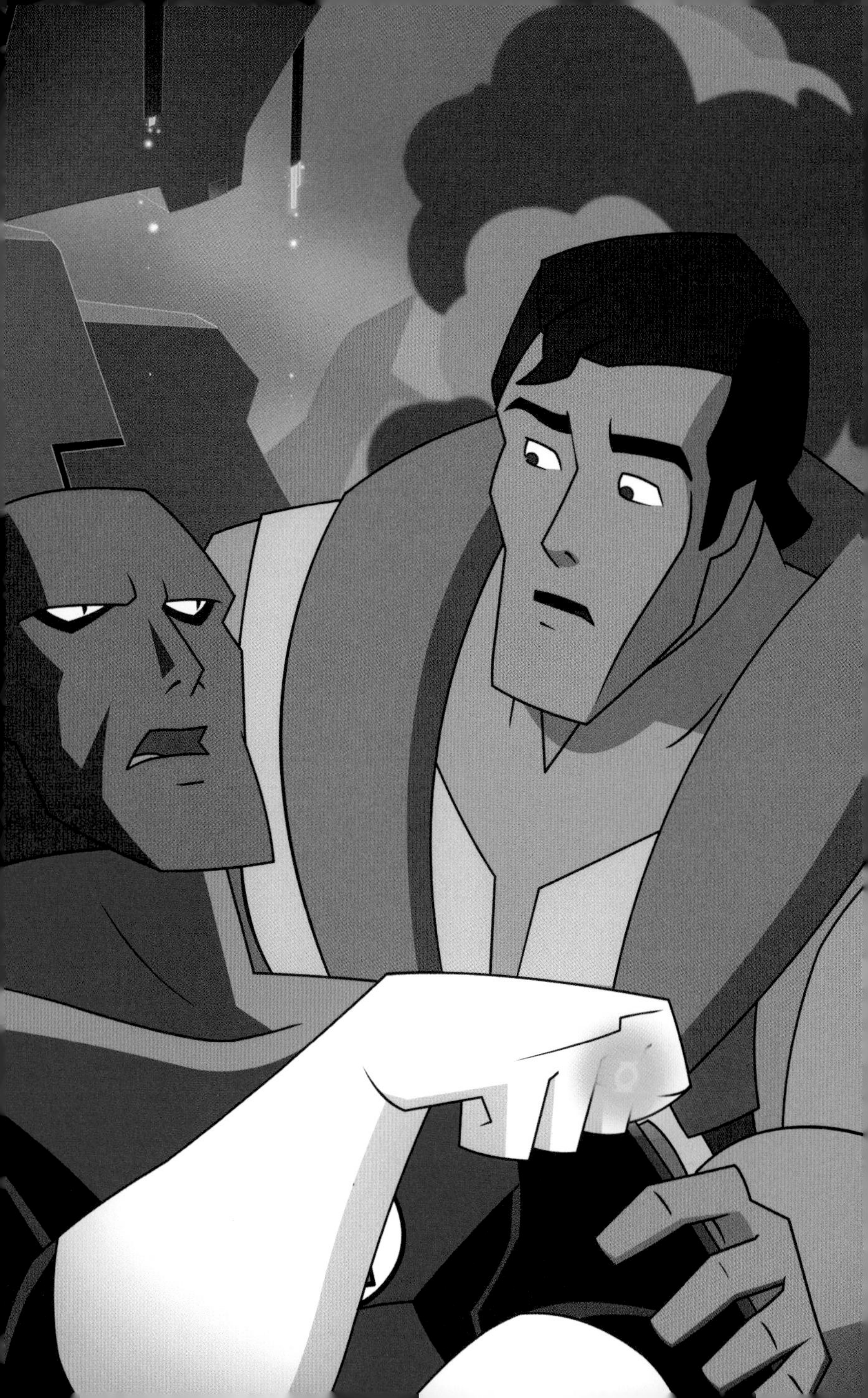

Abin Sur shook his head. "The only person who can help me right now is *you*, Hal Jordan." The alien stared directly at the human pilot. "To be more accurate," he said, "it is the *universe* that needs your help."

Hal looked at the alien. He glanced at his own jet, resting on the ground behind him. Then he turned back to Abin Sur. "Yup. I'm sure I must be dead," said Hal.

Abin Sur raised his right fist. On one of the alien's knuckles glowed a green ring.

"This ring is what saved you and your ship," said Abin Sur.

"That green glow I saw came out of that ring?" asked Hal.

"A Green Lantern's power ring," said Abin Sur.

"I belong to the Green Lantern Corps." Abin Sur gestured to his uniform. "We protect the universe from evil and tyranny. We restore peace and harmony to the planets. And now that I am about to die, I must find my replacement. A warrior to take my ring. That replacement is you, Hal Jordan."

"I'm no warrior," said Hal.

"You are a man who can overcome great fear," said Abin Sur. "Your will is strong. Your heart is pure."

"I wish you'd tell that to my mother," said Hal.

"I do not have much time left," Abin Sur said. He reached behind him and lifted up a strange device. It reminded Hal of an old-fashioned railroad lantern.

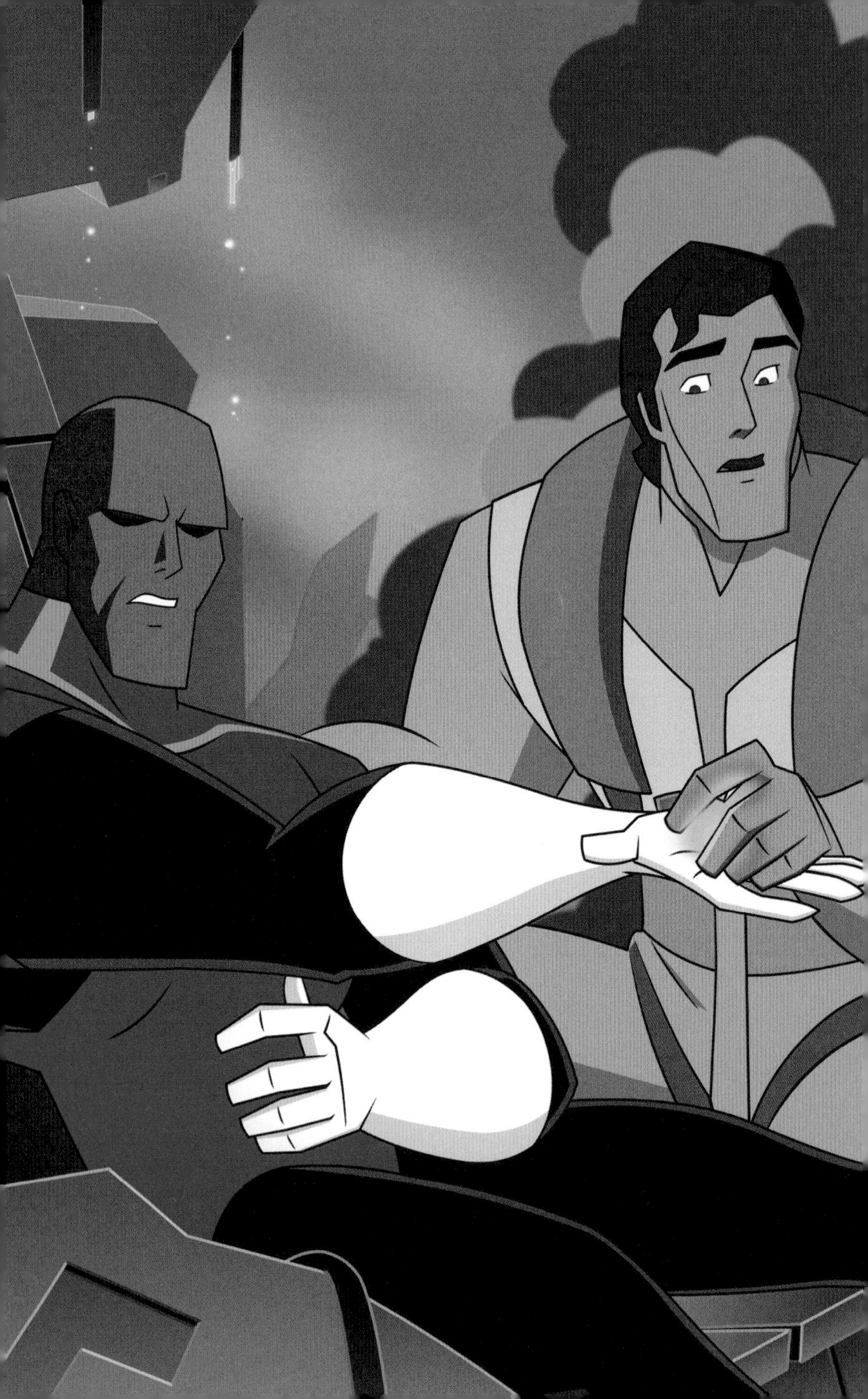

"This is your power unit. It will energize your ring," Abin Sur said with a cough. "You must keep it charged, ready for any situation."

Hal stared at the injured alien. "I don't understand," he said.

Abin Sur nodded. "You will," he replied. "The ring is never wrong." He pulled it off his finger and offered it to the test pilot. "Take it," he said. "It is yours now."

For some reason, Hal did not hesitate. He picked up the ring and held it in his fist. A vibration raced down his arm and shook his entire body.

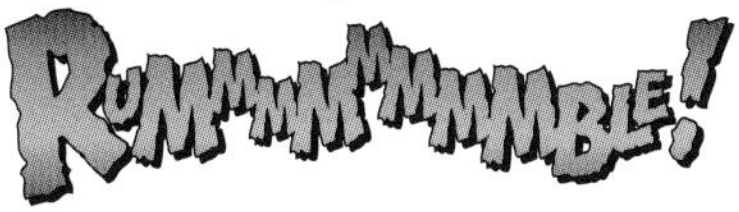
RUMMMMMMMMMBLE!

The alien ship began to tremble. The sand beneath the two pilots shifted and shuddered.

"Hal Jordan," called out Abin Sur. "You must become the guardian of Sector 2814. You must become the Guardian of Earth and the other planets."

"But how do I —?" Hal began.

The green ship sent out a wave of heat. The Earthman stumbled backward. He felt as if the door to a furnace had suddenly opened in front of him.

Hal was blinded by a blaze of white light.

CHAPTER 4

POWER RING

When Hal Jordan opened his eyes a full minute later, he was alone. The green ship lay quietly on the desert sand. The creature that called himself Abin Sur had vanished.

I must be dreaming, he thought. *Carol was right. I should never have taken off my helmet. Now my brain doesn't have enough oxygen, and I'm flying a jet at 41,000 feet. I have to find the controls.*

Hal clenched his fist. Something small and hard was resting inside.

He opened his fingers and saw the green ring that the alien had given him.

"Well, it certainly feels real," Hal said to himself.

He picked up the ring with his other hand and examined it. It felt light and cool to the touch. The air around the ring was blurry and wavy, as if the ring were super-heated. "I might as well see if it fits," he said.

Hal placed the green band on the middle finger of his right hand. Then he flexed his fingers a few times.

"Guardian of Earth, huh?" he said. "I don't feel any different —"

He was surrounded by green flame!

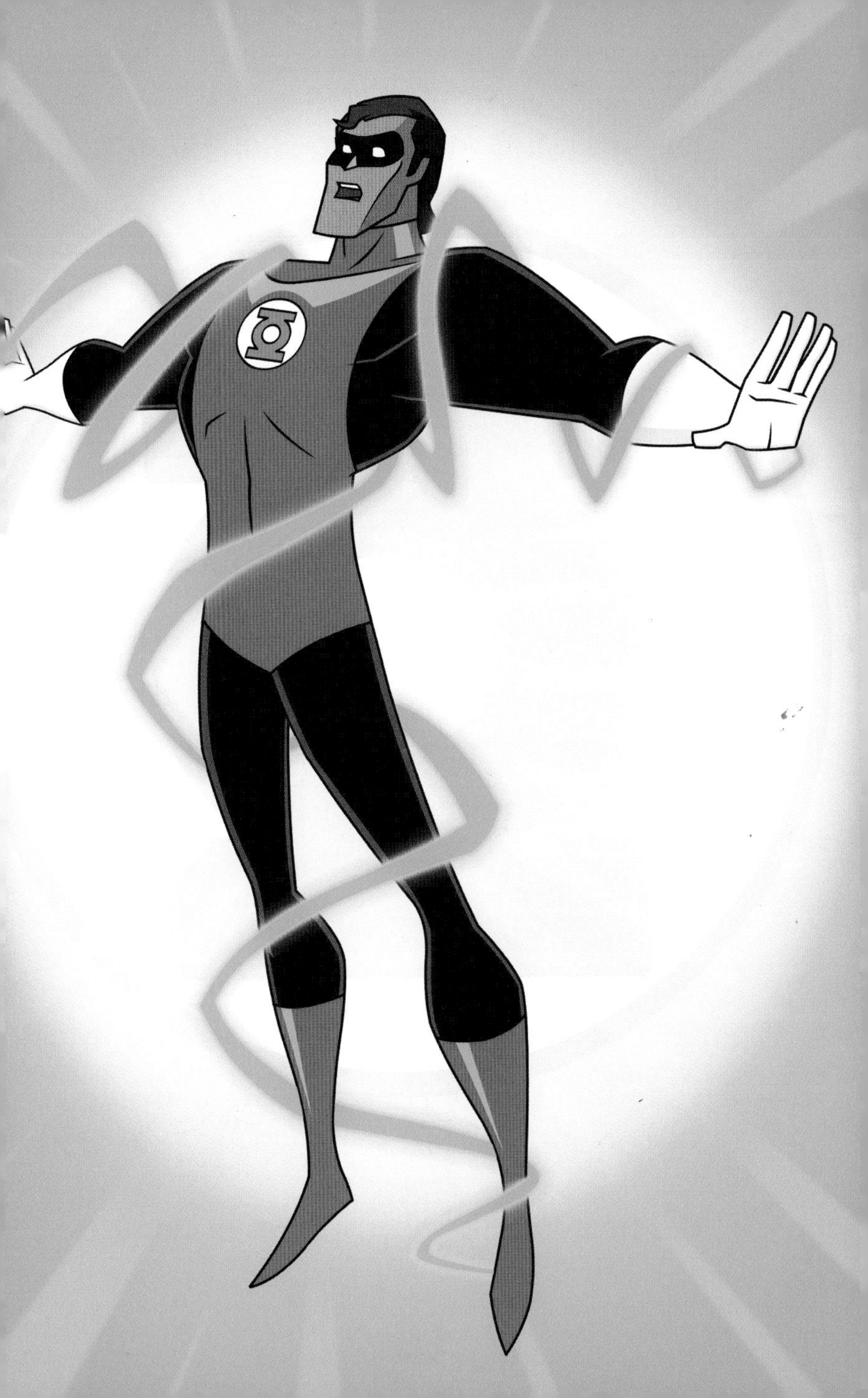

The green fire gathered into long strings and ribbons. The ribbons of emerald energy swirled around his body. Weird images raced through his mind.

Hal felt as if he were flying across the galaxy. Faster and faster he soared. Past icy planets and meteor clouds. Past purple and orange nebulas of mind-numbing size.

Onward he flew to the very heart of the universe. And there he saw a world full of living creatures. The creatures were of every size and color and shape. But each one wore a black and green uniform. They had come from every planet and every galaxy. They were all flying, just as he was, toward a giant structure shaped like the power unit given to him by Abin Sur. It was a colossal green lantern.

Hal heard all the aliens begin to chant.

They each spoke in their own language, but he could understand them all. The chant began: *In brightest day, in blackest night . . .*

Then the planet and aliens disappeared. Once more, Hal was standing in the desert on Earth. His body felt like it was on fire. His hand, the one with the ring, seemed lighter than air. When he looked at the ring, it no longer felt like a separate object. Now it was part of his body, like a muscle or joint or bone.

Hal's flight suit was gone. He was wearing a version of the black and green uniform that all the aliens wore. Abin Sur had called them the Green Lantern Corps.

That's what I am, thought Hal. *I'm a Green Lantern. But what do I do now?*

Hal glanced at his ship. "Carol is probably wondering where I am," he said. "Ha! I don't even know where I am."

Then Hal looked down at his new ring. "The alien called this a power ring. Does it have the power to take me back to Ferris?"

Hal felt a cold breeze flowing across his body. His feet were no longer touching the ground. He was flying. Flying without his jet. His body soared above the red desert. The green ring seemed to pull him through the sky.

"What?!" he cried. "This isn't possible!"

Suddenly, he found himself descending toward the ground. "Uh, maybe it is possible," he said aloud. He stopped descending. He hung motionless in the air.

"Let's go faster!" he decided.

Suddenly, Hal sailed away from his damaged ship, eastward through the air. Hal realized that the ring responded to his every thought! He banked through the air. He skimmed above the rocks and sand. He zoomed in loops and circles with the speed of a missile.

He was flying so fast that he didn't notice the approaching mountains. *I'm gonna crash!* he thought. Instinctively, Hal aimed his ring at the mountain and thought of a tunnel being created.

ZZRRRRTT! A beam of green light shot from the ring and carved a passage through the rock. Hal flew through the mountain to safety on the other side.

Next, he flew straight up into the sky, hovering among the clouds. Then he plunged down like an Olympic diver.

When he was only a few yards above the ground, he halted, turned, and landed gently on the soles of his emerald boots.

The ring had placed him back where he had started. His stalled jet lay on the sand a few hundred yards away.

"All right," he said. "I know how to get back to base. But somehow I need to get the jet back, too. Hmm, the jet's frame is made out of steel. . . ."

Moments later, Hal was flying again. He was heading toward the line of buildings on the horizon. This time, a stream of green light stretched from his ring, trailing below him like a cable. Hal glanced down and smiled. A giant green magnet extended from the end of the cable. And secured to the magnet was his jet.

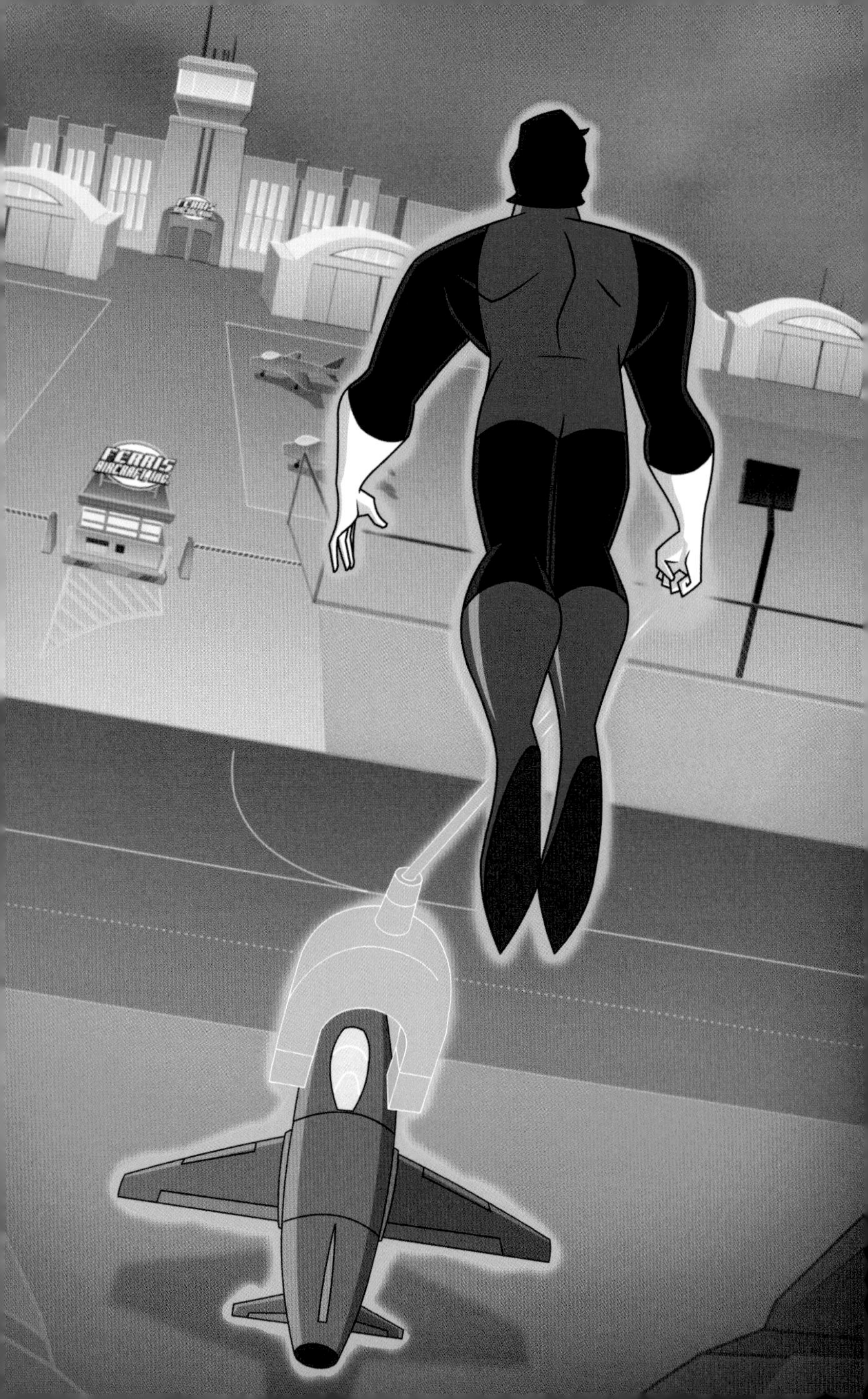
FERRIS
AIRCRAFT INC

CHAPTER 5

GREEN LANTERN

That night, Hal sat alone in his apartment. The green ring lay on the desk in front of him.

Earlier, when he had arrived at the Ferris airfield, he placed the aircraft in the nearby hills. He commanded the ring to cover his new uniform with his former flight suit. Then he walked the few miles back to the airbase. He told Carol and the rest of the staff that he had flown the jet back with only one engine. He told them that the jet had flown low to the ground.

That was why they hadn't seen it on their radar, he explained. But why hadn't he told the truth? For some reason, Hal knew he had to keep the story of the Green Lantern a secret. It was too important to share with anyone — not now, anyway.

As he stared at the ring, he remembered Abin Sur's last words: "You must become the Guardian of Earth."

But how? Hal wondered.

The ring grew brighter. Then the walls in his apartment began to shimmer like a heat mirage. Hal grabbed the ring and shoved it onto his finger.

The air around him began to swirl. Papers blew off his desk. Chairs fell over. A wall clock fell to the floor.

Then everything stopped.

Standing in front of Hal was a stranger who looked as if he had stepped out of a sci-fi movie. He was thinner than a normal human being. His face was sharp and cruel. His skin was almost purple.

He's wearing a uniform like mine, thought Hal.

Something else about the stranger looked familiar. He reminded Hal of the weird vision he had when he first put on his new power ring. In fact, Hal noticed a similar power ring gleaming on the stranger's right hand.

"Another Green Lantern club member? Sorry, I don't know the secret handshake," said Hal.

The stranger did not look friendly.

Hal grinned. "You could have knocked first," he said.

"You are a fool," said the stranger in cold English.

This guy's not like the other one, thought Hal.

"Indeed, I am not," said the stranger aloud.

Swiftly, Hal held out his fist. With the speed of thought, he shot a blast of energy at the intruder.

Faster than the blast, the intruder surrounded himself with a green protective bubble. *Force field,* thought Hal. He had read about them in his science fiction novels.

"Very cool," said Hal. He told himself to use that trick sometime.

The stranger aimed his own ring at Hal. A beam of light hardened into a robotic arm. A robot hand reached toward the Earthman's neck.

Hal figured he couldn't shoot into the force field bubble, but he could attack from a different direction. As the green robotic fingers brushed against his skin, Hal shot another energy blast. This time he aimed at the floor.

The floor's support beams caved in. The stranger was thrown off balance. The robotic arm twisted away. That gave Hal just enough time to imagine himself flying through the night sky.

Instantly, he was soaring above the buildings of Coast City. He was no longer wearing his jeans and T-shirt. Once more he was dressed in a Green Lantern uniform.

The intruder flew after him. "Who are you anyway?" Hal shouted.

Instantly, the cruel-looking stranger was in front of him. He aimed his ring at Hal.

Emerald shackles gripped the Earthman's wrists and ankles. He was held motionless among the clouds, unable to escape. He was unable to make his ring fire again. His willpower was no match for the stranger's.

"Hey, I thought we were on the same team," said Hal. "Members of the Green Lanterns Corps, right?"

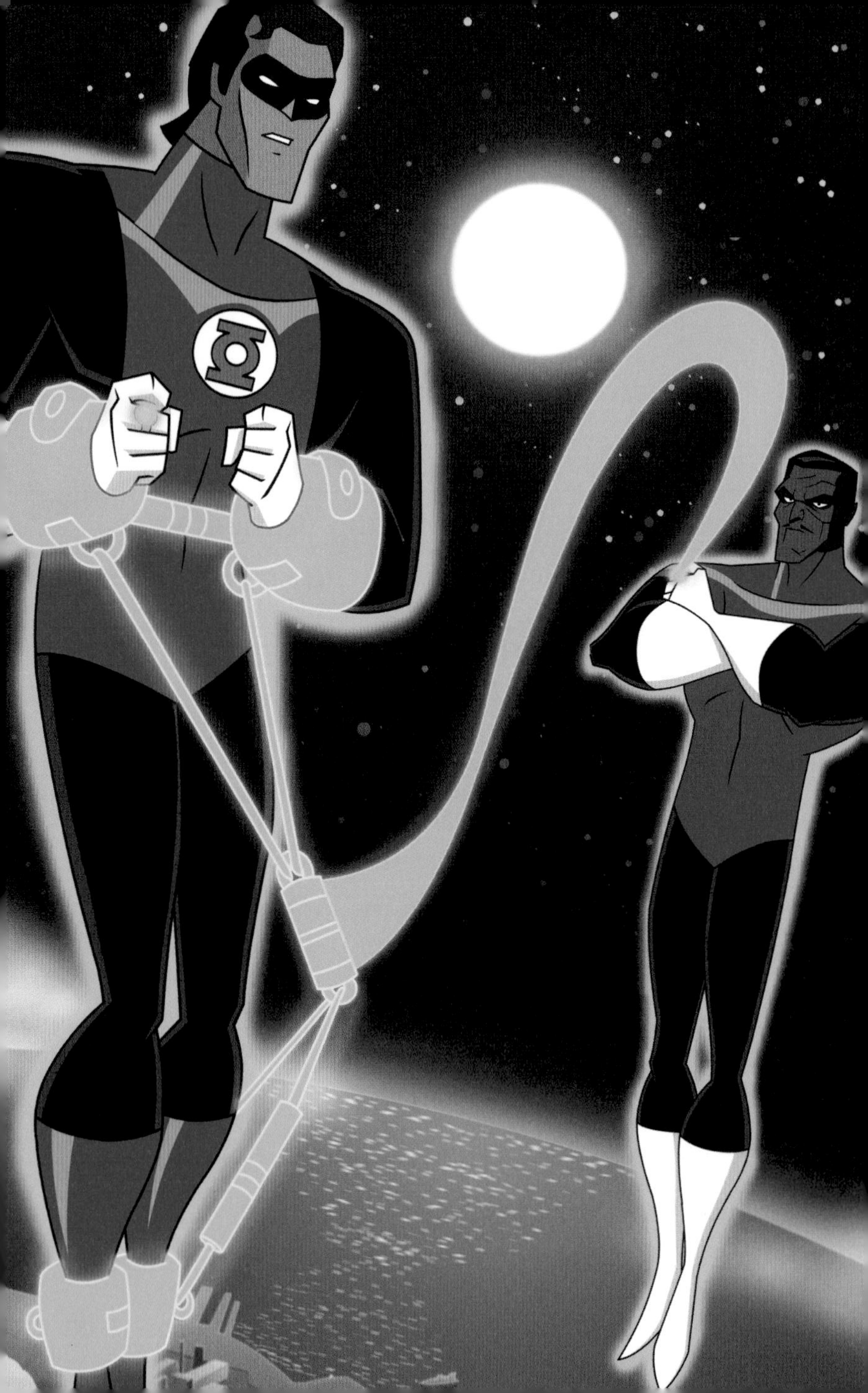

The purple-skinned warrior answered, "You attacked first."

"I had an E.T. in my living room," said Hal. "What was I supposed to do?"

The stranger shook his head. "I told the Guardians they were wrong. You humans are violent and unpredictable. You are dangerous to others and to yourselves. You should not be wearing Abin Sur's ring."

"He gave it to me," said Hal. "I didn't steal it, if that's what you're thinking."

The stranger hovered closer to Hal. "I know exactly what happened," he said. "I know that Abin Sur sought you out. And I know the ring chose you."

"So, what's with the rough treatment?" asked Hal.

The stranger sneered.

"You have no idea of a Green Lantern's power," he said. "A ring has never been worn by an Earthling before."

"There's a first time for everything," said Hal.

A grim smile spread over the stranger's lips. "You're not a coward, I'll say that much for you." Then the man flashed his ring. "Or are you?"

The shackles holding Hal in place disappeared. Instantly, he plummeted back toward the surface of the Earth. His body jerked and twisted as the cold air whipped past him.

"This is . . . just like . . . testing that G17 twin-engine last summer," Hal said, through chattering teeth. He closed his eyes and concentrated on his ring.

Slowly, his body came to a halt. Once more, he hovered among the clouds.

A blast of green lightning shot past him. Hal turned and ordered his ring to create a huge green bubble to cover him.

"Ha ha ha ha!" The stranger appeared next to him, chuckling.

"What's going on?" demanded Hal.

"Excellent reflexes," said the stranger. "And you used the force bubble that you saw previously. Good memory. I think you might be worth training after all."

"Training?" repeated Hal. "And I suppose you're my trainer?"

"The best," said the alien. "I am Sinestro, a member of the Corps."

"That is the purpose of my visit," Sinestro continued. "I was sent to find you and train you. To begin your journey as a Green Lantern. That is, if an Earth creature can possibly be worthy."

Even though Sinestro's words were not evil, Hal sensed something mean and hard about the warrior.

"When do we start this journey?" asked Hal. "And by the way, the name's Hal Jordan — not Earth Creature."

Sinestro glared at Hal again. "To answer your question: We leave for Oa tonight."

Oa? A picture flashed through Hal's brain. He saw the planet filled with aliens from his previous vision.

"The journey will be long," said Sinestro. "Where is your power unit?"

Hal remembered the strange device that Abin Sur had given him. He commanded his ring to fly him back to his apartment. Once there, he used the ring's power to repair the broken floor. Then, as he fetched the power unit, Sinestro came through the wall of his living room.

"I don't think I'll ever get used to that," said Hal.

He set the unit on a table. Sinestro stepped closer. Hal was about to ask what he should do next, but he didn't need to. In the presence of another Green Lantern, somehow he knew just what to do. It was second nature for him to raise his fist and hold his ring to the power unit.

The two warriors' rings touched the unit as it glowed brightly.

ZZRRRRRTT!

Green energy radiated throughout the room. The two men began to chant. It was the same chant that Hal remembered from his vision. This time, he too was speaking the words . . .

In brightest day,
In blackest night,
No evil shall escape my sight.
Let those who worship evil's might,
Beware my power —
Green Lantern's light!

The two warriors slipped like shadows through the walls of Hal's apartment. They flew straight up into the sky.

Hal Jordan smiled. He knew that he was taking the first step in the greatest adventure of his life. Becoming a Green Lantern — and the Guardian of Earth.

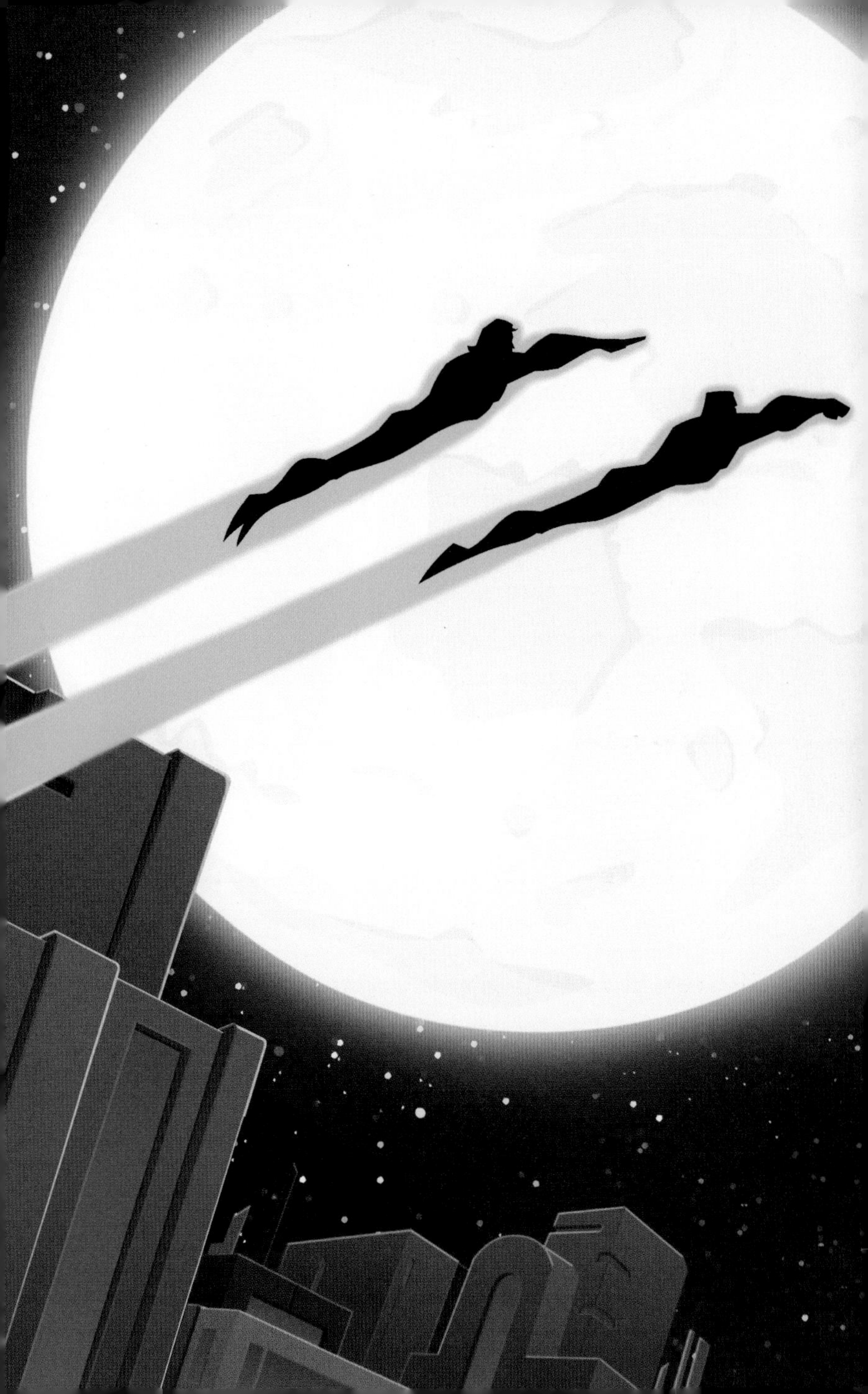

ABIN SUR

BIRTHPLACE: Ungara

OCCUPATION: Green Lantern

HEIGHT: 6' 1"   **WEIGHT:** 200 lbs.

EYES: Blue   **HAIR:** None

POWERS/ABILITIES: Unmatched willpower; ring creates hard-light projections of anything imaginable; ring can translate any language.

BIOGRAPHY

On his home planet, Ungara, Abin Sur was a professor of history. At an early age, he was appointed by the Green Lantern Corps to be the Guardian of Sector 2814. Soon, he made history of his own taking on powerful enemies. While on patrol, a villain known as Legion attacked Abin Sur's space ship. He made an emergency landing on Earth and one final heroic act — Abin appointed Hal Jordan as his replacement.

Each Green Lantern patrols a specific area of space called a sector. Abin Sur guarded Sector 2814, which included Earth. After Abin Sur's death, Hal Jordan took control of this sector.

Abin Sur did not decide who would be the next Green Lantern — his ring made this decision. It believed Hal Jordan had the strength and will to become a powerful member of the Corps.

The Green Lantern Starkaor recruited young Abin Sur into the Corps. Starkaor patrolled Space Sector 2814 until he was killed by the villain Traitor.

After Abin Sur's death, his only son, Amon Sur, joined a group of criminals known as the Black Circle. He eventually became a member of the Sinestro Corps, powerful enemies of the Green Lanterns.

BIOGRAPHIES

Michael Dahl is the author of more than 200 books for children and young adults. He has won the AEP Distinguished Achievement Award three times for his non-fiction. His Finnegan Zwake mystery series was shortlisted twice by the Agatha awards. He has also written the Library of Doom series and the Dragonblood books. He is a featured speaker at conferences around the country. He has written other origin stories for the DC Super Heroes series, including *The Last Son of Krypton, The Man Behind the Mask,* and *Trial of the Amazons.*

Dan Schoening was born in Victoria, B.C., Canada. From an early age, Dan has had a passion for animation and comic books. Currently, Dan does freelance work in the animation and game industry and spends a lot of time with his lovely little daughter, Paige.

ORE NEW
REEN ANTERN
VENTURES!

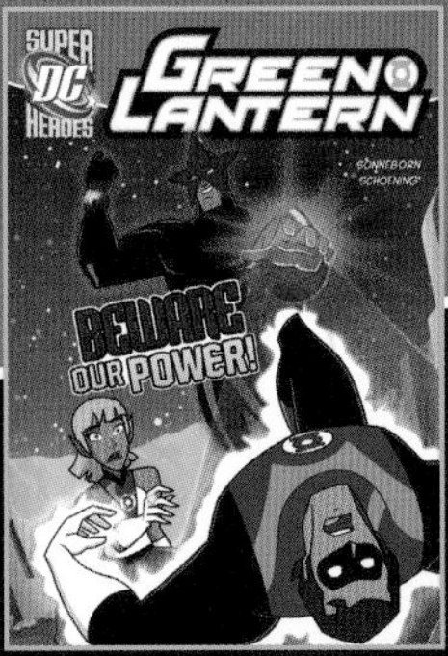
SUPER DC HEROES
GREEN LANTERN
BEWARE OUR POWER!

BEWARE OUR POWER!

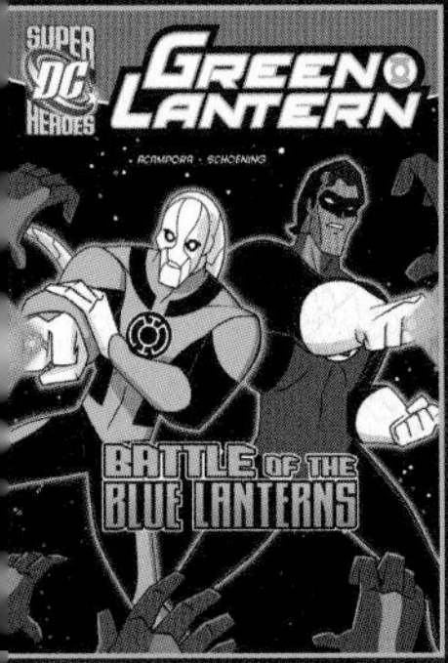
SUPER DC HEROES
GREEN LANTERN
ACAMPORA · SCHOENING
BATTLE OF THE BLUE LANTERNS

TLE OF THE BLUE LANTERNS

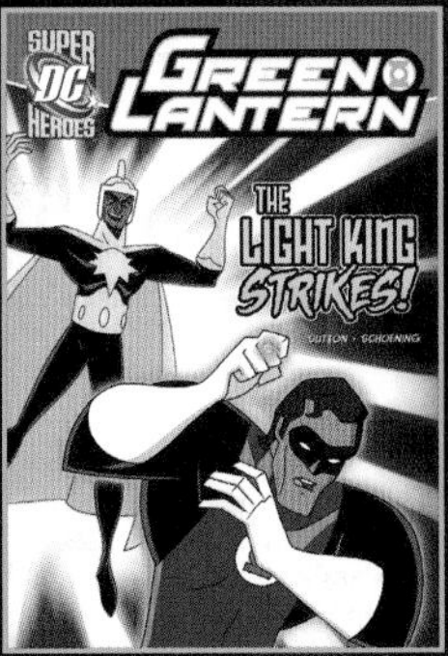
SUPER DC HEROES
GREEN LANTERN
THE LIGHT KING STRIKES!

THE LIGHT KING STRIKES!

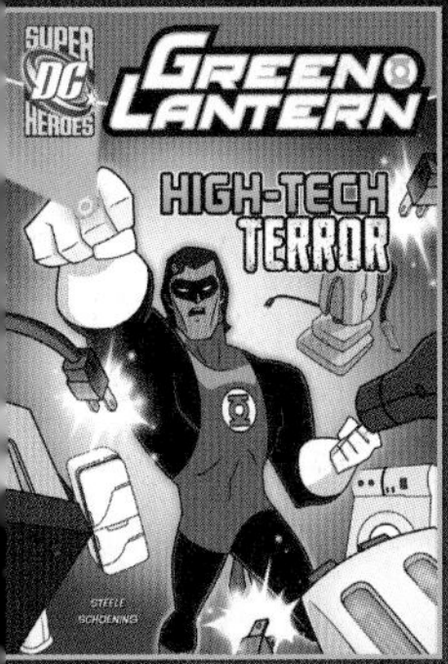
SUPER DC HEROES
GREEN LANTERN
HIGH-TECH TERROR

HIGH-TECH TERROR

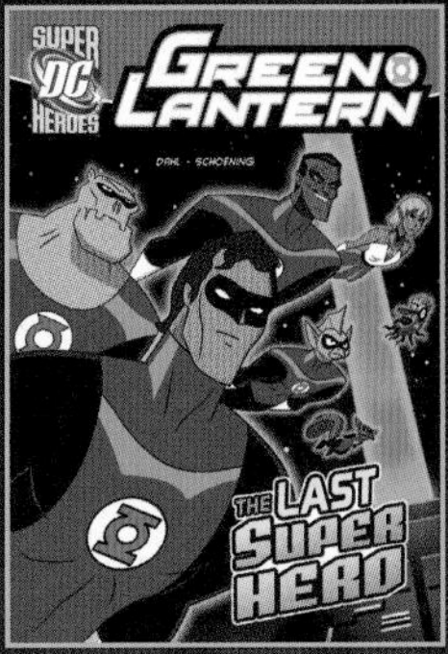
SUPER DC HEROES
GREEN LANTERN
DAHL · SCHOENING
THE LAST SUPER HERO

THE LAST SUPER HERO

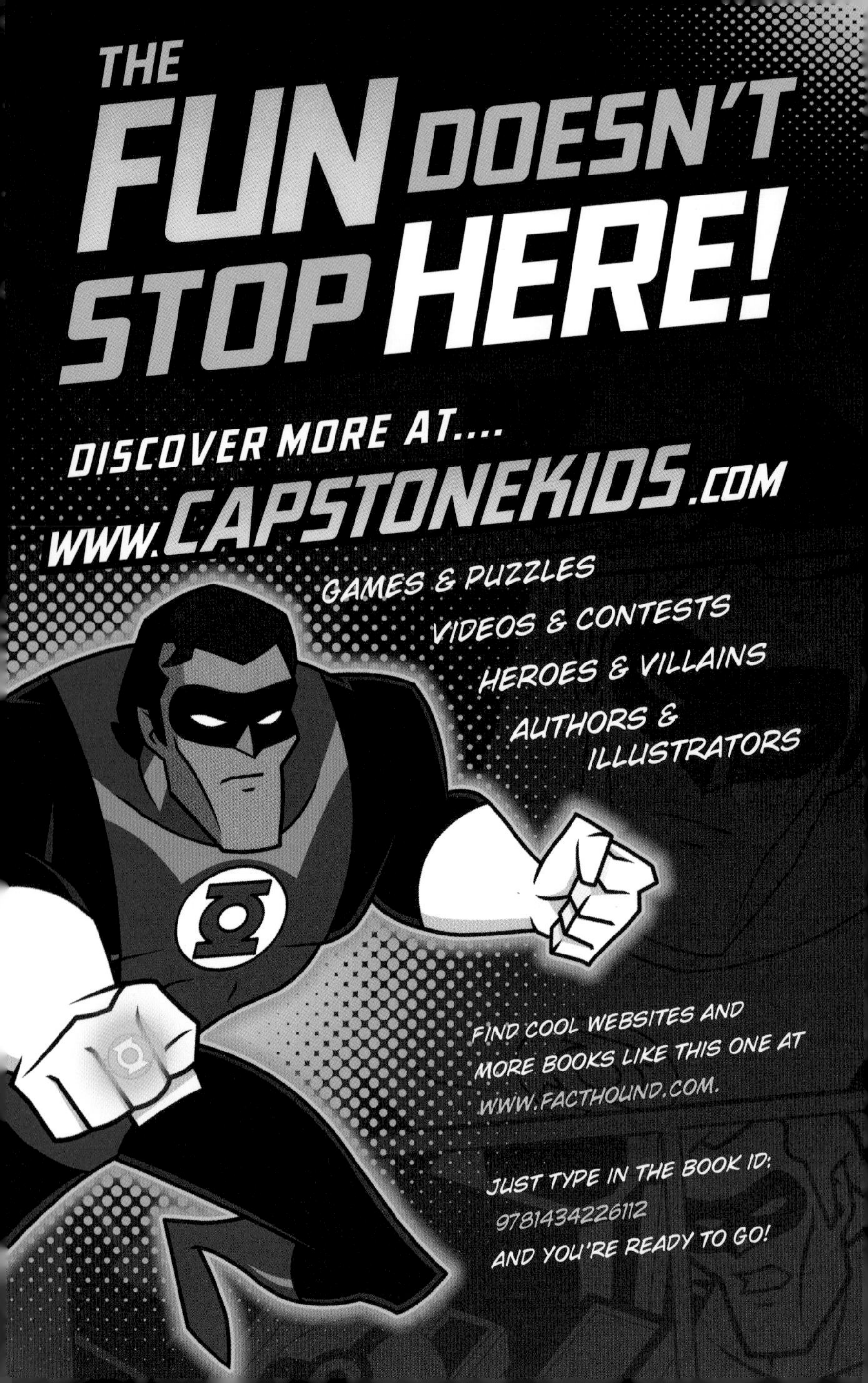
THE FUN DOESN'T STOP HERE!
DISCOVER MORE AT....
WWW.CAPSTONEKIDS.COM
GAMES & PUZZLES
VIDEOS & CONTESTS
HEROES & VILLAINS
AUTHORS & ILLUSTRATORS
FIND COOL WEBSITES AND MORE BOOKS LIKE THIS ONE AT WWW.FACTHOUND.COM.
JUST TYPE IN THE BOOK ID:
9781434226112
AND YOU'RE READY TO GO!

DISCUSSION QUESTIONS

1. When Hal accepted the Green Lantern ring, he took on a great responsibility. Do you have any responsibilities? How do you handle these tasks?

2. Why do you think Sinestro didn't like Hal Jordan? Do you think they will ever get along? Explain your answer.

3. If you could travel to any planet in the solar system, where would you go? Why?

WRITING PROMPTS

1. Write your own Green Lantern adventure. Where will Hal go next? What evil villains will he face? You decide!

2. The Green Lantern ring can create anything the wearer imagines. If you had a ring, what would you imagine it to create? Write about your creation, and then draw a picture of it.

3. Members of the Green Lantern Corps come from all different planets. Create your own Green Lantern. What planet does it come from? What does it look like? What is its name?

GLOSSARY

altimeter (al-TIM-uh-tur)—an instrument that measures how high something is above the ground

ancestor (AN-sess-tur)—a member of a family who lived a long time ago

atmosphere (AT-muhss-fihr)—the mixture of gases that surrounds a planet

cockpit (KOK-pit)—the front section of a plane where the pilot sits

corps (KOR)—a group of people acting together

guardian (GAR-dee-uhn)—someone who guards or protects something

nebula (NEB-yuh-luh)—a bright cloud of stars, gases, and dust that can be seen in the night sky

orbit (OR-bit)—the invisible path followed by an object circling a planet

tyranny (TIHR-uh-nee)—the ruling of people in a cruel or unjust way

willpower (WIL-pou-ur)—the ability to control what you will and will not do

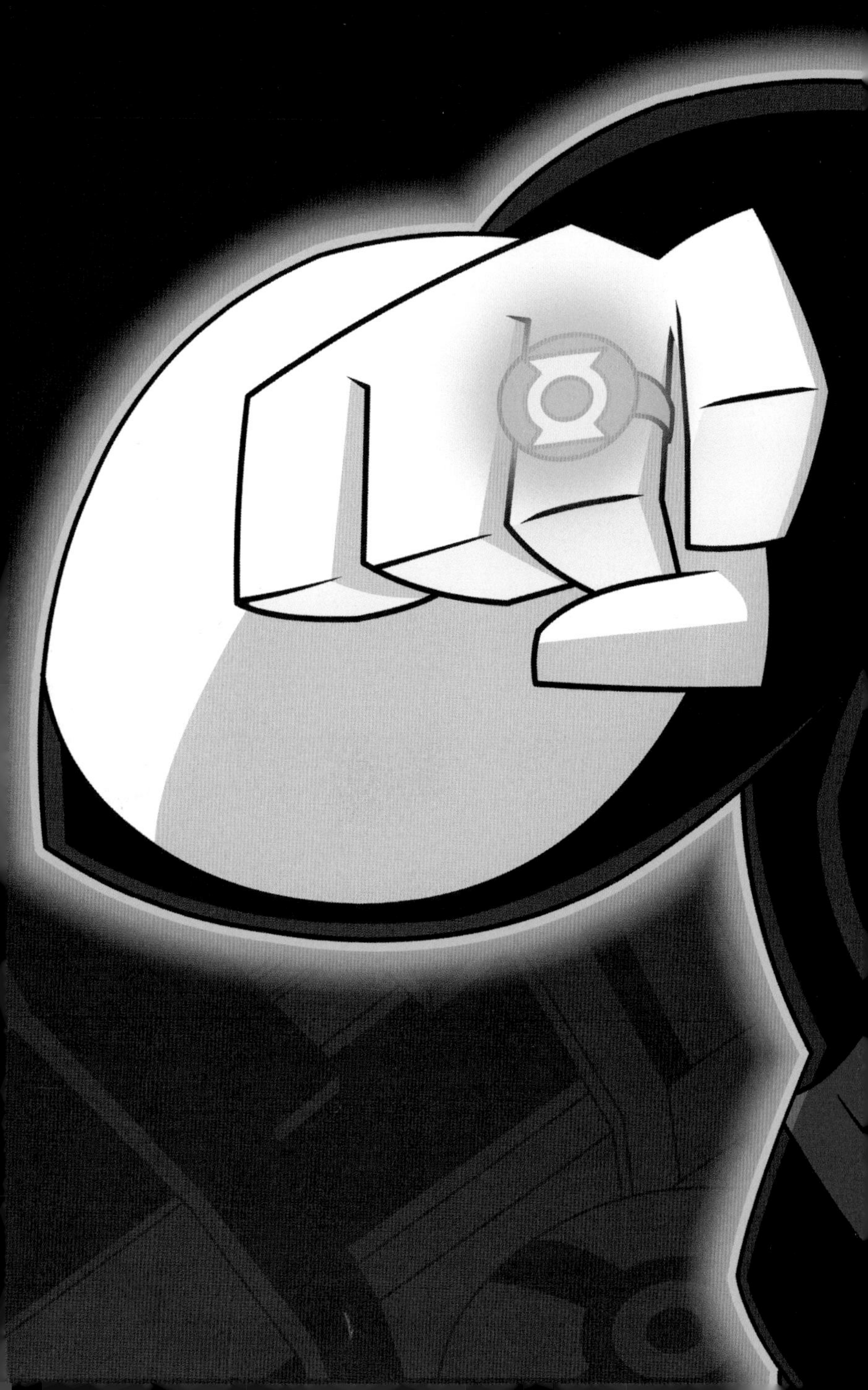

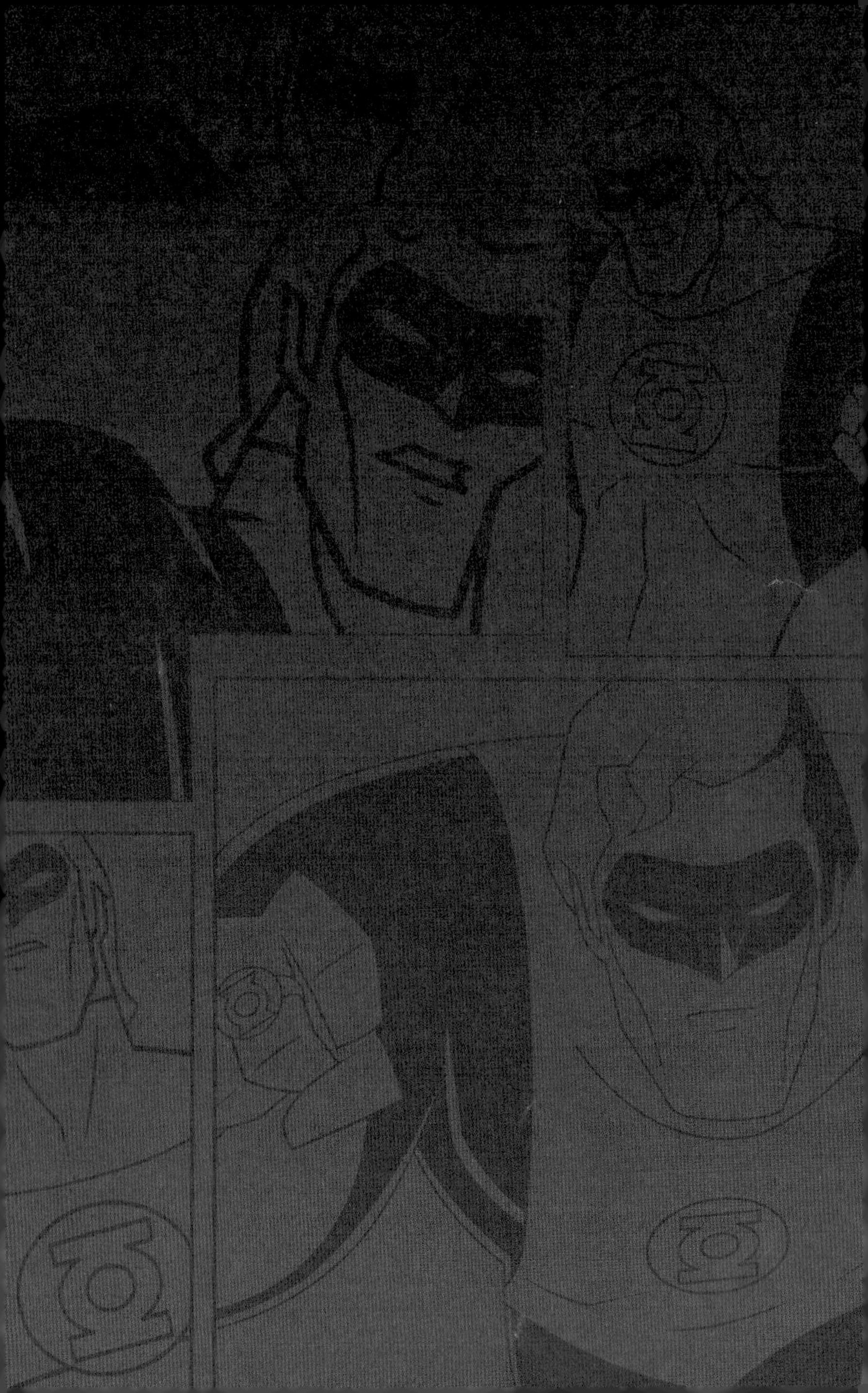

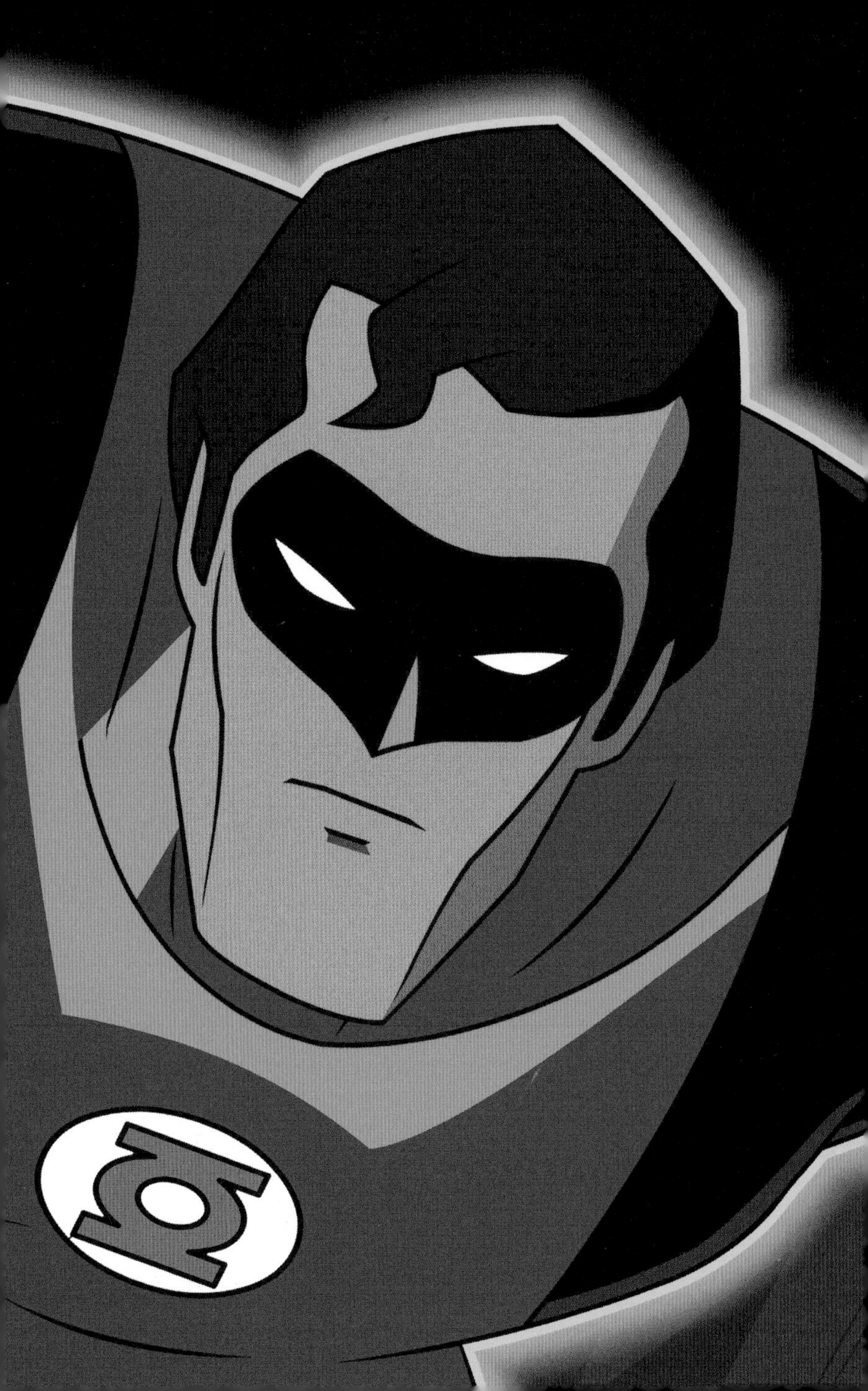